Trust Reba

Trust Reba

written and illustrated by

JOSEPH LOW

McGraw-Hill Book Company

New York • St. Louis • San Francisco • Düsseldorf • Johannesburg
Kuala Lumpur • London • Mexico • Montreal • New Delhi • Panama
Rio de Janeiro • Singapore • Sydney • Toronto

3456789 RABP 797876

Library of Congress Cataloging in Publication Data

Low, Joseph, date
    Trust Reba.

    SUMMARY: Though chaos seems to result when Reba,
the family bear, takes on more and more chores,
the family realizes she does deserve their love and
trust.
    I. Title.
PZ7.L9598Tr   [E]   73-17418
ISBN 0-07-038838-5
ISBN 0-07-038839-3 (lib. bdg.)

Once there was a family who lived in the forest.
They were much like the other families of the time, but
they were different in one special way.

    They kept a bear.

She had come to them out of the woods on one of
those warm days which sometimes happen late in winter.

They had given her food and a bed by the fire,
thinking that when spring came she would return to
the forest.

But by the time spring did come, she was a member of the family. She ate with them at the table and had her own dish and spoon which the father had carved from a block of pine wood.

She wore an apron made specially
for her by the old aunt.
She even had a name: R E B A.
The mother had made it up
by rearranging the letters of
the word B E A R. And the children
had embroidered it on the apron.

She had learned to sweep
the floor with a broom.

She could carry water
from the well

and wood for the fire.

And she was good at washing clothes. The big
wooden tub would be filled with water, clothes, and
enough soap. Then Reba would climb in and begin to
stamp her big feet up and down, sloshing all together
till the clothes were clean.

It is true she could not talk, but she would listen carefully and make soft grunting sounds to show that she understood, or that she was pleased, or that she was puzzled.

In the evenings they would all sit by the fire. The father would carve things with his knife and tell old jokes. The mother and the old aunt, busily sewing clothes for the new baby's christening, would tell stories. The children would chatter about this or that, and they would all gossip about the people in the neighboring village.

At times, in a quiet moment, they could hear Reba in her corner, making small happy rumbles deep in her chest, her eyes half closed as she rocked gently back and forth. She loved the family and they loved her— more and more.

As the days went by, they came to count upon her help. She was a bit slow at her work, to be sure. She would frown and breathe heavily, but that was only because she was trying so hard to do it right.

And she was very dependable. When she swept the floor, it was spotless. When she brought wood for the fire, it was stacked in a neat pile with no chips or bits of bark scattered about. And no water ever spilled from the buckets she carried.

When, as a final measure of their love and confidence, the family allowed her to watch over the baby in his cradle, she rocked it gently back and forth with one great paw: never too hard, never too fast.

In fact, she was so reliable in everything she did, they came to use an expression, "Trust Reba!" meaning "You can count on her for sure."

As spring came on, the family became more and more excited about the baby's christening, soon to take place in the village church. For weeks they had been preparing special food for the great day, all made strictly according to the old recipes they had always used—and their parents and grandparents before them.

Most important of all was the wine, which was put in a great glass bottle that was kept only for christening feasts.

At last the great day came! The family rose with the
sun, put a fine embroidered cloth on the long trestle
table and set out the food in its many dishes and bowls.
In the midst of it all, glowing in its straw-covered bottle,
was the wine.

As they left for the church, the mother carried the
baby in his fine new clothes.

At the door the father turned to Reba and said solemnly
(though he meant it half in joke),

"Keep the house and all in it safe from rogues till we return."
  Shuffling her feet, the bear nodded and rumbled, looking very serious. And she waved goodbye as they disappeared among the trees.

Then she patrolled outside the house, searching the
woodpile, the hen house, the pig sty, and the cow barn
to make sure that all was well.

She did the same inside, inspecting the cupboard,
the closets, the big chest, and under the beds. All was
in good order: nothing to worry about.

So she sat down in the father's big chair to rest, rocking gently back and forth in the warm sun beside the window. Soon she began to nod. Outside the birds twittered; inside a fly hummed in the chimney.

But suddenly, half asleep, half awake, she heard a most alarming sound: a loud, angry buzzing sound. She leaped to her feet and stumbled about the room, her eyes blurry, yet careful not to bump the table with its lovely burden of food.

Then at last she did see something clearly: a large bee landing on the wine bottle.

"Aha, you rogue," cried Reba. "Would you steal our baby's precious wine?" With a fierce swipe of her paw she missed the bee but struck the bottle, splashing wine over the food and the tablecloth.

The bee flew out the window.

Reba stood dumbfounded. She could hear the family
returning through the woods.

"Look," cried the father. "A bee! A good omen!
Our baby will be a fine worker."

"Right," said the mother. "Busy as a bee. It's an old
saying."

They were all hungry from their long walk and they chattered happily about the good things they would soon be eating, and the wine in its great straw-jacketed bottle.

Only the old aunt, always a worrier, said, "Oh dear, I do hope nothing has gone wrong."

"What could go wrong on our baby's christening day?" said the mother.

"Didn't we leave a good guard on the house?" said the father. "Trust Reba!"

But as they entered the house and saw the table, they were horrified. "I told you," cried the old aunt. "Didn't I tell you? I told, but who listens?"

Poor Reba was driven out in disgrace and the family all rushed about trying to clear things up.

After a while, when they had got over their excitement and anger a little, they were surprised to find that although the food was sprinkled with wine, it could still be eaten. And much of the wine was still in the bottle.

"But this tablecloth is a mess," said the mother. "We can't eat here. Come, we'll take everything out under the trees."

"Yes," said the father. "In the fine warm sun. Let nothing spoil this day!"

"A picnic," shouted the children.

"With bugs?" said the old aunt.

So they were all themselves again, and they trooped outdoors, carrying the food and the wine. Soon they were gaily eating and laughing together. They even discovered that in some cases the wine made the food taste much better. Each urged the others, "Try this! Like you never had it so good. We must add wine to the old recipe."

In their delight, they forgot the bear.

When they had gone from the house, Reba crept back and looked at the empty table and the wine-stained cloth. What could she do? She gathered up the cloth and carried it to the big tub behind the house. She fetched water, put in soap, climbed into the tub and began to tramp with her big feet.

Slowly at first, the cloth, the water, the soap and the feet went s-l-o-s-h, s-l-o-s-h. But as she went on, Reba began to feel better. She was doing a good thing to wipe out a bad one. So she pumped her feet up and down, faster and faster: slosh,slosh,slosh,slosh!

It made a very loud noise: so loud it carried clear around the house. When the family heard it, they were alarmed. They could not see what was happening.

"What now," cried the old aunt. "A flood she's making?"

They all rushed to the house and around in back.

Reba stopped tramping and stared at her feet, terrified
that she must, again, have done something wrong.

And the family, with nothing to say for once, stared
first at Reba, then at each other. They were ashamed of
what they had done to their friend.

But suddenly the father gave a loud, happy shout:
"Such a bear! From bad she brings good. Trust Reba!"
    And they all gathered around the tub to help her
rinse the big tablecloth and spread it to dry on the
grass. Then they led her to the picnic and began to
stuff her with goodies.

Reba gobbled, wept, smiled, and rumbled altogether.
Her big red tongue licked crumbs from one corner of
her mouth and tears from the other.

All were happy again. The mother took the baby,
put him in the bear's great lap, kissed her on the nose,
and cried,

"Trust Reba!"